Five reasons why you'll love Isadora Moon...

Meet the magical, fang-tastic Isadora Moon!

Isadora is half vampire, half fairy, totally unique!

Discover what might happen if your snowman came to life!

Visit the magical ice palace!

Enchanting pink and black pictures

What do you like to do when it snows?

Throw snowballs
at my brother!
– Leila

I like catching the
snowflakes with my tongue.
– Rayhan

I lie on the floor and wave
my arms up and down to
make wings like Isadora has!
– Millie

Make a snow fort!
– Sophie

Sledging down the
biggest hill!
– Nyla

I like looking for
monster footprints
in the snow.
– Lewis

Family Tree

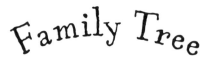

My Mum
Countess Cordelia
Moon

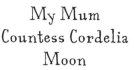

Baby Honeyblossom

My Dad
Count Bartholomew
Moon

Pink Rabbit

Me!
Isadora Moon

For vampires, fairies, and humans everywhere!

And for the wonderful team at
OUP Children's Books.

OXFORD
UNIVERSITY PRESS

Great Clarendon Street, Oxford OX2 6DP

Oxford University Press is a department of the University of Oxford.
It furthers the University's objective of excellence in research, scholarship, and
education by publishing worldwide. Oxford is a registered trade mark of Oxford
University Press in the UK and in certain other countries

British Library Cataloguing in Publication Data

Data available

ISBN: 978-0-19-276868-1

1 3 5 7 9 10 8 6 4 2

Printed in China

Paper used in the production of this book is a natural,
recyclable product made from wood grown in sustainable forests.
The manufacturing process conforms to the environmental
regulations of the country of origin.

ISADORA · MOON

Makes Winter Magic

Harriet Muncaster

OXFORD
UNIVERSITY PRESS

Chapter ONE

It was a cold and frosty Monday morning and I was making my way to school with Pink Rabbit hopping along beside me. It was so chilly that I could see frozen spiderwebs twinkling in the morning sunshine, and, when I breathed, white clouds puffed into the air. That is why we were both wearing our knitted scarves and

woolly hats with bobbles on them.
Of course, Pink Rabbit doesn't really
feel the cold because he is made of
stuffing, but he still likes to dress up.
He used to be my favourite cuddly toy
but my mum magicked him alive for me
with her wand. She can do things like
that because she is a fairy!

When we got to school I could see that there was something very interesting happening in the middle of the classroom because all my friends were gathered there in a little group.

'Oliver's having a party!' said Bruno, waving a colourful invitation around in the air. 'Ice-skating!'

'Ooh!' said Zoe, craning to see. 'I've never been ice-skating before!'

'Me neither!' I said excitedly. 'I can't wait!'

But after a few minutes we realized that Oliver had already handed out all his invitations and now he was standing there looking a bit flustered. His cheeks had gone bright red.

'I'm sorry,' he said, shrugging. 'I was only allowed to invite three friends. Ice-skating is expensive.'

'Oh,' said Zoe disappointedly.

'That's a shame,' said Sashi, trying not to sound hurt.

I stared down at the floor and didn't say anything. My cheeks were burning and I felt embarrassed for thinking that I would be invited.

'I really am sorry,' said Oliver. 'I wish I could have invited everybody!'

'Don't worry,' said Zoe, patting him

on the arm. 'We understand.'

'Yes,' agreed Sashi. 'We do! Don't we, Isadora?'

'Of course!' I squeaked quickly.

For the rest of the day I tried very hard not to think about Oliver's party, but by the time I got home in the afternoon it was still on my mind.

'What's the matter?' Mum asked as she put my peanut-butter sandwich snack down in front of me. 'You're very quiet today.'

'Too quiet,' said Dad, yawning. He had just woken up. My dad is a vampire so

18

he sleeps through the day and stays up all night.

'It's nothing,' I said.

'Nothing!' said Dad. 'Rubbish! If it was nothing you would have eaten all of that disgusting peanut-butter sandwich by now!' Dad thinks all food is gross unless it is red.

'Well,' I began. 'It's just that my friend Oliver is having a party. And he didn't invite me.'

'That's a shame,' said Mum, who was busy mashing up an avocado for my baby sister, Honeyblossom. 'But you know, we can't all be invited to everything, I'm afraid.'

'Mum's right,' agreed Dad. 'Don't take it personally, Isadora. I'm sure Oliver didn't want to hurt anyone's feelings.'

'I know,' I said. 'I'm sure he didn't. I just feel a bit disappointed. He's going ice-skating! I've never been ice-skating before. I would love to try it.'

'Ah!' said Mum. 'My sister and I used

to have such fun ice-skating on magical ice
rinks in the forest clearing. Nature is so
beautiful when it's all twinkly and frosty!'

'Aunt Crystal, you mean?' I said.

'Yes,' said Mum. 'She used to magic
the most amazing ice rinks for us with
her wand. Her speciality is ice
magic, remember? Because she
was born in the winter.'

'I know,' I said. 'She's a
snow fairy. I wish you were
a sparkly snow fairy, Mum!'

'I don't!' said Dad,
wrapping his cape tightly
about him. 'Brr!'

'I much prefer being

a summer fairy,' said Mum. 'Flowers
and sunshine are my speciality!' She
started to spoon the mashed avocado
into Honeyblossom's mouth and
Honeyblossom spat it right out again.

'Thinking about it,' said Mum, 'we
haven't seen Aunt Crystal for a long time.
Maybe I should invite her over for the
weekend?'

'Really?' said Dad, wrapping his cape even more tightly around himself. 'Must we? She makes the house so *cold*.'

'Yes!' said Mum firmly. 'It's important to see family. I'll give her a call on the crystal ball later. You can always hug a hot-water bottle.'

'Humph,' said Dad.

'Woo hoo!' I said.

Chapter TWO

The following weekend, at exactly two o'clock, there was a sharp *rat-a-tat-tat* on the front door. I ran to open it and a gust of snowy air blew into the hallway.

'Isadora!' cried Aunt Crystal, pulling me towards her for an icy hug. She looked more beautiful than I had remembered. Her long silvery hair floated out around her head and sparkled with tiny snowflakes. In her hand she was holding a suitcase that looked as though it was made of ice.

'I'm so glad you're here, Aunt Crystal!' I said, taking her suitcase from her and then putting it down quickly because it was so cold.

'It's lovely to see you again, my darling!' trilled Aunt Crystal. 'It's a change from my cosy little igloo at the North Pole. There's not much snow around here, is there?'

'No,' I said. 'I wish there was! Mum was telling me all about how you used to go ice-skating together when you were little.'

'Oh yes!' said Aunt Crystal. 'We used to have such fun! Have you ever been ice-skating before, Isadora? Everyone should try it at least once!'

'I haven't,' I said, thinking enviously of Oliver's party again. 'Some of my friends are going ice-skating today for Oliver's birthday party but I didn't get invited. It's expensive.'

'It is,' agreed Aunt Crystal, 'if you go to the big ice rinks in the city. But it's not at all expensive if you're a snow fairy like me! Let's go to the back garden!'

I took her hand excitedly and led Aunt Crystal to the back door. She threw it open and we both peered out into the wild garden. Aunt Crystal raised her wand and . . . SWISH!

Snowflakes glittered and sparkles

fizzed. In the middle of our garden was a hard, shiny mirror, glinting in the sunlight. It looked a bit odd surrounded by the green grass. Aunt Crystal must have been thinking the same thing because she waved her wand again and this time the whole garden turned into a winter wonderland. Frost twinkled on branches and snow lay thickly all over the ground. The air felt different—cold and quiet and muffled.

'There,' said Aunt Crystal. 'I feel more at home now.'

'It's beautiful!' I whispered.

Just then Mum and Dad came up behind us.

'Hello, Crystal!' cried Mum happily, pulling her in for a tight hug. 'I see you've already found the garden. Look at all those glinting icicles!'

'Brr!' said Dad, rubbing his hands.

'A snow day!' I yelled, racing back inside to get my coat and boots and gloves.

Mum dug out her old ice skates and then magicked some up for everyone else, except Honeyblossom who was too little to ice-skate. Dad put on his warmest woolly vampire cape and Aunt Crystal went around the house flinging open all the doors and windows.

'It's nice to have a cool breeze in the house,' she said.

'An arctic breeze, more like!' complained Dad, clutching his woollen cape tightly around himself.

Then we all went outside. Aunt Crystal taught Pink Rabbit and me how to glide across the ice rink. Pink Rabbit was a little unsure because his paws kept

sliding all over the place. Dad watched
from the edge, shivering.

'Come on, Bartholomew!' said Aunt
Crystal. 'You're missing out on the fun!'

'You'll like it, Dad!' I yelled, twirling
clumsily around on my ice skates. 'It's
like flying!'

Eventually Dad stepped tentatively onto the rink. He put one foot in front of the other and slid onto the ice. Then he held out his cape so it billowed around him, and skated a bit faster.

'Oh!' he said in surprise. 'I'm a natural after all!'

After a while, Mum, Aunt Crystal,
Honeyblossom, and Dad went inside, but
Pink Rabbit and I stayed in the garden. I
wished some of my friends were with me
but Zoe and Sashi had not been free and
Oliver was busy having his party. I
wondered if it had started yet and what
sort of cake he would be having. It made
me feel a little bit sad, so I decided to
make a snowman to cheer myself up.

'Come on, Pink Rabbit,' I said,
starting to make a ball with my hands.
'You can help!' I put the ball on the
ground and started to roll it so that it got
bigger and bigger. 'This will be the body,'

I said. 'Do you want to make the head?'

But Pink Rabbit wasn't interested in helping me. He was making his own little snowman. A snow bunny!

I started to make the head on my own and then I searched around the garden for something to use for eyes and buttons. I found some dark pebbles buried in the snow by the flowerbed so I poked them into the snowman's head and chest. I thought he still needed something else, so I ran inside and fetched one of my capes which was hanging up behind the front door. It was my favourite one with stars and moons all over it. It fitted my snowman perfectly.

'Hmm,' I said. 'I think he's too small to be a snowman. I think he's a snow boy!'

I stood back to admire my handiwork and Pink Rabbit stood back to admire his. My snow boy looked so friendly. He had a big wide smile that I had drawn into the snow with my finger. I beamed back at him.

And then he winked! I jumped
backwards in shock.

'Pink Rabbit!' I said. 'Did you see that?'

Pink Rabbit nodded excitedly. He
lifted his paw and waved it at his snow
bunny. When the snow bunny waved back,
Pink Rabbit bounced up and down with
glee. The snow bunny sprang away across
the garden and Pink Rabbit began to hop
after her. They were playing
chase!

I stared hard at my
snow boy, and as I did
so he started to move his
head, slowly, as though he was
testing out his neck. As though he had

never used it before.

'It must be the magic snow!' I breathed. 'The magic fairy snow!'

I watched in wonder as the snow boy started to come to life. He lifted one of his arms into the air and waved it. Then he lifted a leg and stepped out onto an untrodden bit of snow. His cape blew out behind him and started to billow around, sending flurries of glistening snowflakes into the air.

I lifted my hand to wave.

'Hello!' I said. 'I'm Isadora.'

'Isadora,' said the snow boy. 'What's that?'

'It's my name!' I told him. 'I'm a

vampire fairy. And you're a snow boy!'

'Snow Boy,' said Snow Boy. 'Is that my name then?'

'It can be!' I told him. 'If you want it to be.'

'I like it,' said Snow Boy. He stared all around at the white sparkling garden and at Pink Rabbit and the snow bunny bounding around.

'That's Snow Bunny,' I told him. 'She's made of snow too. Just like you!'

'Just like me!' said Snow Boy with a smile. Then he stepped towards me, his frosty feet crunching over the glittering blanket of snow. I held my hand out to him and he took it.

'I'm so happy I've got someone to play with now!' I told him. 'None of my friends were free today, and the rest of them were at a party. They went ice-skating.'

'Ice-skating,' said Snow Boy wonderingly. 'That sounds like fun. What is it?'

'Let me show you!' I said. 'I think you would like it!' I held out my pair of ice skates for him to put on. He undid the laces and peered inside. Then he put them on his hands.

'Not like that, Snow Boy!' I laughed, showing him how to put them on his feet properly. I led him to the ice rink and Pink Rabbit and Snow Bunny came hopping over. Snow Bunny immediately leapt onto the ice, skidding across it on her snowy paws and doing a pirouette. Pink Rabbit watched from the edge. I think he was afraid of making a fool of himself.

I showed Snow Boy how to put one foot in front of the other and how to glide across the ice. It was a bit difficult without ice skates and I kept falling over.

'Here,' said Snow Boy, taking the skates off and handing them back to me. 'You wear these. I don't need them.'

'Are you sure?' I asked. But Snow Boy had already leapt back onto the ice, his frosty feet slipping and sliding across the rink.

We spent a long time whirling and twirling across the ice and Snow Bunny did lots of showing off. Eventually our legs started to get tired so we stepped off the rink and back onto the snow. It was quite late now and starting to get dark outside.

'What's that?' asked Snow Boy, pointing up at my house where light glowed from the windows. 'It looks big.'

'That's my house!' I laughed. 'Where I live. Would you like to see it?'

Snow Boy nodded so I led him across the garden and through the back door into the kitchen. Mum, Dad, and Aunt Crystal were not there but Aunt Crystal's wand was lying on the table.

'They must be in the sitting room,' I said. 'But I'll introduce you to them later. Would you like to see my bedroom first?

I've got lots of toys we can play with!'

'I've never seen a toy before!' said
Snow Boy, but he sounded excited.

'Follow me!' I said, and together we
ran up the stairs, Pink Rabbit and Snow
Bunny hopping happily along behind us.

Chapter THREE

'Wow!' said Snow Boy when we finally got up to the top of the tallest turret where my bedroom is. 'We're so high up!'

'We can see the whole town from here,' I said, pointing out of the window.

I showed Snow Boy some of my favourite things. I showed him my doll's house and my magic mermaid necklace, given to me by a real mermaid, and my star diamond tiara, given to me by a real ballet dancer.

'It's so sparkly,' said Snow Boy, putting the tiara on his head and twirling around. 'Like ice!'

'It *does* sparkle like ice!' I said, watching him hold it up in the air. He put it down again and then moved over to my bookcase.

'What are these things?' he asked. 'They look interesting.'

'They're books!' I told him, getting excited.

'They are full of stories and different worlds! Let me show you my favourites!' I knelt down and began to flick through some of my books, showing him the pictures and characters inside.

'This is such fun!' said Snow Boy. 'I want to read them all!'

'That would take a long time,' I said. 'But we can try! Maybe we can act out some of the stories too, with Pink Rabbit and Snow Bunny!'

'I would love that,' said Snow Boy happily. 'You have such good ideas. It's so much fun playing together!'

I beamed at the compliment, feeling all glowy inside. I loved playing with Snow Boy too. I wanted him to stay forever! But then I noticed something that made me start to worry. When Snow Boy moved his hand to turn a page, little drops of water came flying off him and little drips and puddles were beginning to appear all over my books and the floor.

'Oh dear,' I said. 'Snow Boy, I think you're melting!'

'Melting?' said Snow Boy. He looked confused.

'Hang on,' I said, reaching for my wand, which was sitting on my bedside table. 'Let me try and freeze you again.' But when I waved my wand nothing happened.

'I'm not sure my wand has snow magic in it,' I said. 'Maybe we should go back outside again.'

Snow Boy looked disappointed. 'Can't we just stay in here a little longer?' he begged. 'I want to finish looking at this book.'

'Why don't we take it outside?' I suggested. But Snow Boy had already started turning the pages and was busy stroking the illustrations, making them all wet. When he finished he jumped up and ran over to my wardrobe. He flung the doors open, threw off his cape and started trying on all my clothes.

'I think we should go outside now,'
I said, feeling panicked at the trickles of
water that were now starting to run off
Snow Boy's legs. He was too busy trying
on my hats to hear me.

I tried to think quickly. How could I
stop Snow Boy from melting in the house?

A vision of Aunt Crystal's
wand lying on the kitchen
table floated into my mind.

'Wait here!' I said to
Snow Boy. 'I'll be back
in a minute!' I flew down
the stairs as fast as my
wings could flap and into
the kitchen. The wand

was still on the table. I grabbed it and raced back upstairs.

I'm sure Aunt Crystal won't mind, I thought, though a tiny part of me felt a bit guilty for not asking.

When I got back to my bedroom I noticed that Snow Boy didn't look quite so chirpy. He was hopping up and down and looking worriedly at his melting feet that were splashing into puddles on the floor. Snow Bunny had her head poking out of the window, trying to keep cool.

Quickly I waved the wand in the air and imagined that my whole bedroom

had turned to ice. Snowflakes and glitter flurried around as I swooshed it about. My arm fizzed with electricity—this wand felt much more powerful than mine! Things began to happen fast. My bed started to frost over and my floor turned hard and shiny like an ice rink. Icicles began to grow from my ceiling and suddenly it got very, very cold. I felt like we were inside a freezer and I was very glad that I was still wearing my coat.

'That feels better!' said Snow Boy, breathing a sigh of relief. He wiggled his leg out in front of him and this time no water dripped off it. He opened up the front of my doll's house and started

to play with the things in there. I knelt down beside him and started to play too. I felt so happy I had managed to stop my new friend from melting that I forgot all about putting Aunt Crystal's wand back. We pretended to be giants in a world of tiny people and we were having so much fun that it took a while before I heard the shouts coming from down below, getting closer and closer towards my bedroom door.

'Isadora!' came my Dad's voice through chattering teeth. 'Is this your doing?'

'Where's my wand?' came Aunt Crystal's panicky voice.

'What is going on?' cried Mum.

I looked up guiltily and saw Mum,
Dad, and Aunt Crystal standing at my
bedroom door. They didn't look very
pleased.

'I just did a little bit of snow magic,' I said in a small voice. 'To stop Snow Boy from melting!'

'You've turned the whole house into an ice house!' said Mum. 'My lovely plants and flowers are all frozen. They'll die!'

'We're slipping all over the floor!' complained Dad. 'I've already fallen over twice!'

'Honeyblossom can't sit in her high chair!' wailed Mum. 'It's too cold and icy for her!'

'Where's my wand?' asked Aunt Crystal.

'It's here!' I said, handing it to her and starting to feel upset. 'I'm really sorry. I didn't think you'd mind. I was just trying to stop my snow boy from melting. I only meant to freeze my bedroom! I didn't realize it would freeze the whole house!'

'This wand is very powerful,' said Aunt Crystal. 'You shouldn't have taken it without asking. It could have been dangerous.'

'I'm sorry,' I said again. 'I really am.'

'Well, don't do it again,' said Aunt Crystal. 'You should always ask before borrowing other people's things.'

'I know,' I said in a small voice. 'I won't do it again.'

Aunt Crystal smiled and put her hand on Snow Boy's shoulder. 'Is this your new friend?' she asked. 'Did you make him from my magic snow?'

'Yes I did!' I said. 'And Snow Bunny too!' I pointed at Snow Bunny who was now happily bounding around my bedroom. Pink Rabbit wasn't looking quite so happy as his paws were skidding all over the place.

'We've been having such fun together,' I said. 'We wanted to keep playing in my bedroom. Snow Boy wanted to see my things.'

'I did!' said Snow Boy, standing up now and bowing. 'Everything is so interesting here! I love it! And I love playing with Isadora.'

'I love playing with Snow Boy!' I said. 'I don't ever want him to melt. I want him to stay forever!'

Mum smiled at Snow Boy but she began to look a bit uncomfortable and Dad looked worried.

'I'm not sure that's possible,' began Mum. 'Magic can't always last forever. Especially when it comes to snow. Even magic snow melts eventually.'

'But—' I felt my eyes begin to fill up with tears and Snow Boy's cheerful smile had vanished from his face '—we can't let Snow Boy melt!' I wailed. 'We just can't!

I'll have an icy bedroom forever! I don't care! Why can't we just keep the snow in our garden all year round?'

'Because the animals and the plants in the garden need different seasons to survive,' said Mum gently. 'And you can't live in an icy bedroom forever. It's not practical, my sugarplum.'

'I'm not living in an icy house,' said Dad firmly.

'But . . .' I sobbed, tears falling from my eyes and plopping onto the floor, turning to ice immediately. Snow Boy looked confused.

'Why is there snow coming from your eyes?' he asked.

'They are tears,' explained Aunt Crystal. 'Isadora cares about you so much that she can't bear to lose you.' She pulled both me and Snow Boy in for a hug. 'Isadora is right,' she said. 'You can't give up on people that you love. I know a place where Snow Boy and Snow Bunny can go, a place where they will never melt.'

'Where?' I asked, sniffing.

'The Land of Ice and Snow,' said Aunt
Crystal, 'where the Snow Fairy Queen
lives. It's a long way from here but I think
you're brave enough to make it. You'd
need a map of the stars to get there, of
course.'

'A map of the stars!' said Dad, perking
up. 'I can help with that.'

Chapter FOUR

We all made our way out of my bedroom and along to Dad's special astronomy tower. He loves looking at the stars and has a special telescope. It is his favourite hobby. Aunt Crystal put her eye to the telescope and peered upwards into the now-darkening sky.

'Mm-hmm,' she said. And then,
'Hmm, hmm.' She got a piece of paper and
began to scribble some little pictures onto
it.

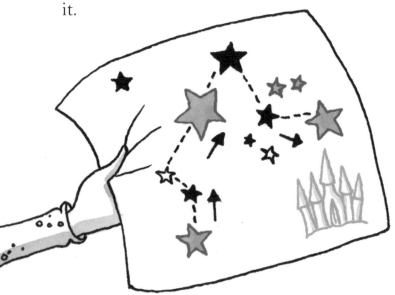

'There you go!' she said, handing me
a map. I stared down at the tiny stars and
then peered through the telescope myself.

I could see exactly where she wanted me to go. There was a trail of extra bright stars leading all the way across the sky. Bravely I stuffed the map into my pocket and took a deep breath.

'I had better get going then,' I said. 'It's going to take a while to get there.'

Snow Boy bit his lip. He looked nervous about going to a new place. He picked up Snow Bunny and hugged her close, stroking her icy fur.

Mum looked worried too.

'You can't go on your own,' she said. 'What if you get lost? I think I should come with you.'

'I won't get lost,' I promised. 'And I

don't need you to come with me.
I made Snow Boy and so it's my
responsibility to get him to the
Land of Ice and Snow. I can do it
on my own.'

'But'—said Mum, wringing
her hands in worry— 'you can't fly
all that way! Your wings are only
small.'

'I agree,' said Dad. 'You'll get
too tired! I should take Snow Boy

myself.' He swished his cape about proudly. 'I am a very speedy flyer!'

'I want to do it!' I said. 'By myself! There must be another way!' I peered out of the window at the snowy garden, which was glowing bright white in the dusky light.

'What if we made a sleigh out of the magic snow?' I suggested. 'One that Snow Boy and I can sit in, that could take us *safely* to the Land of Ice and Snow?' I emphasized the word 'safely'.

'Hmm,' said Dad. 'That could work.'

'It might be a solution,' said Mum.

'I think that's a great idea!' said Aunt Crystal.

★ ★ ★

We all went back downstairs. The garden looked magical in the

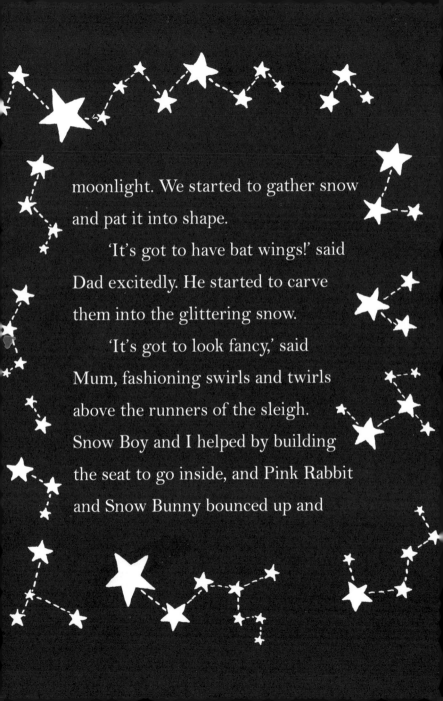

moonlight. We started to gather snow
and pat it into shape.

'It's got to have bat wings!' said
Dad excitedly. He started to carve
them into the glittering snow.

'It's got to look fancy,' said
Mum, fashioning swirls and twirls
above the runners of the sleigh.
Snow Boy and I helped by building
the seat to go inside, and Pink Rabbit
and Snow Bunny bounced up and

down with excitement.

'Magnificent!' said Dad when we had finished and all stood back to admire our handiwork. 'You'll be perfectly safe in that! It's got a steering wheel so you can change direction very easily!'

The sleigh twinkled and sparkled under the light of the fingernail moon and then it started to shudder slightly, juddering this way and that, unsticking itself from the ground underneath. It lifted itself upwards, its big snowy bat wings flapping and sending a shower of flakes into the air.

'I'll get a blanket!' said Mum, hurrying inside to fetch one.

Snow Boy, Pink Rabbit, Snow Bunny,

and I climbed up into the hovering sleigh.

I got the map of the stars out of my pocket

and smoothed it out on my lap, lighting

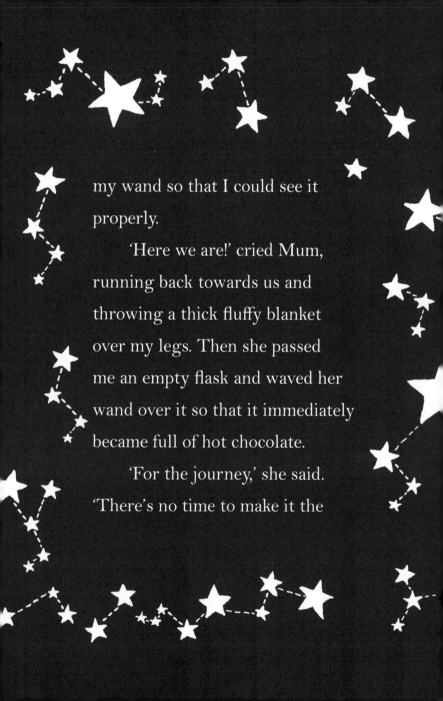

my wand so that I could see it
properly.

'Here we are!' cried Mum,
running back towards us and
throwing a thick fluffy blanket
over my legs. Then she passed
me an empty flask and waved her
wand over it so that it immediately
became full of hot chocolate.

'For the journey,' she said.
'There's no time to make it the

usual way!' Then she passed a raspberry ice lolly to Snow Boy.

'I'm not sure what you eat,' she said. 'But I found this in the freezer.'

'Thank you,' said Snow Boy. 'I'm sure I will love it!'

The sleigh began to rise higher up into the air. Aunt Crystal waved her wand one more time.

'Just to make sure it doesn't melt!' she said.

'Goodbye!' we called, looking over the edge and watching as Mum, Dad, and Aunt Crystal got smaller and smaller and further and further away. Soon they just looked like three tiny dots on the ground and we were soaring still higher, up into the vast twinkling sky.

'That's the star we need to head towards first,' said Snow Boy, glancing down at the map and then pointing to a particularly bright one. He opened his ice lolly and started to lick it.

'Yum,' he said. I steered the sleigh towards the bright star and then opened my flask and took a sip of the hot chocolate. It made my whole body feel warm and glowy and more awake. Mum must have put some fairy magic in there.

'It's so beautiful up here,' sighed Snow Boy. 'And the world looks so small down below.'

'It does,' I agreed, peering over the side and getting butterflies in my tummy. The streets and houses were lit up with tiny lights and the cars looked like toys or tiny insects moving along the roads.

'There's the second star,' I said, pointing at another one, flashing in the distance. 'We need to follow that one now.'

Snow Boy steered the sleigh in

the right direction and we continued to whoosh along, the wind blowing out my hair and Snow Boy's cape.

We flew for a long time through the silent night. Pink Rabbit and Snow Bunny curled up and went to sleep by our feet. We followed star after star, soaring over the glassy sea with its white crested waves and over mountains and lakes and streams.

Eventually the ground below us began to turn white and soon we were in an empty, cold world, covered in glistening ice and snow. There didn't seem to be any humans and the dark sky glowed in all colours of the rainbow, making the snow shine like a kaleidoscope.

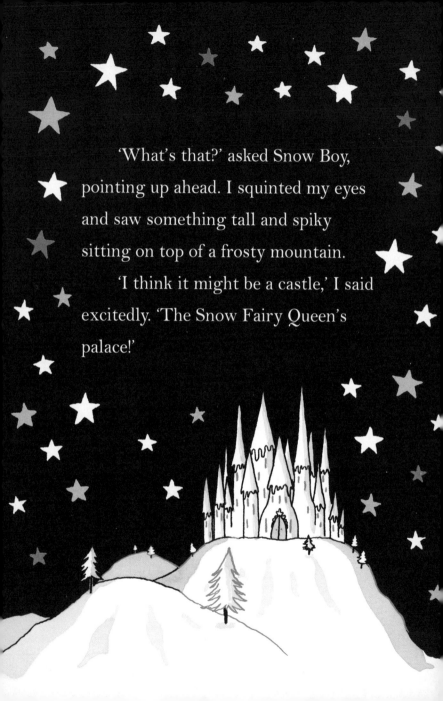

'What's that?' asked Snow Boy,
pointing up ahead. I squinted my eyes
and saw something tall and spiky
sitting on top of a frosty mountain.

'I think it might be a castle,' I said
excitedly. 'The Snow Fairy Queen's
palace!'

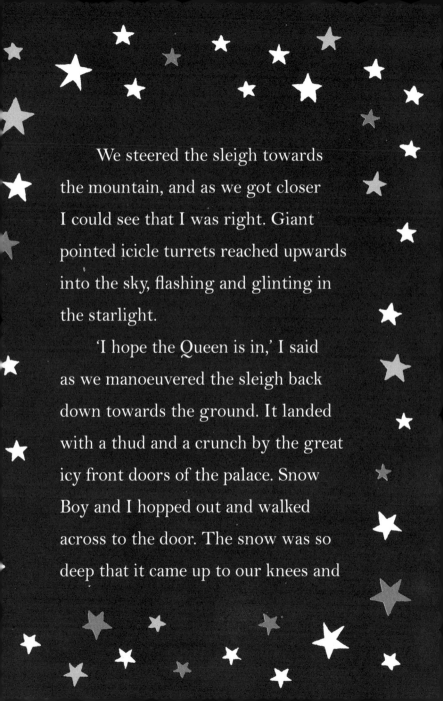

We steered the sleigh towards
the mountain, and as we got closer
I could see that I was right. Giant
pointed icicle turrets reached upwards
into the sky, flashing and glinting in
the starlight.

'I hope the Queen is in,' I said
as we manoeuvered the sleigh back
down towards the ground. It landed
with a thud and a crunch by the great
icy front doors of the palace. Snow
Boy and I hopped out and walked
across to the door. The snow was so
deep that it came up to our knees and

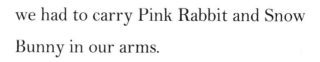

we had to carry Pink Rabbit and Snow Bunny in our arms.

'It feels sort of like home here,' said Snow Boy, taking a deep breath of the freezing cold air. He gazed round contentedly at the snow all around us. It seemed to go on for miles and miles.

I raised my hand and lifted the knocker, clanging it back down on the door. There was a booming sound from inside the palace and suddenly I felt a bit shy.

'I hope she won't mind us dropping in like this,' I said. We stood and waited, and after a few minutes the great doors opened. Standing before them was a friendly-looking snowman wearing a waistcoat.

'Hello?' I said, sticking out my hand like I've seen my dad do. 'My name is Isadora Moon and we've come on business to see the Snow Fairy Queen.'

'On business, eh?' chuckled the snowman. 'Well, you had better come in then! I am the Queen's butler. Follow me.'

We stepped into the great hallway and I tried not to slip on the shiny frozen floor. Above us hung a great chandelier made of snowflakes and icicles that tinkled as we walked under it.

'I should have brought my ice skates!' I whispered to Snow Boy as I skidded and slid across the floor. We followed the butler down a long cold corridor full

of paintings of snow people and then
through a door into another large room.
There was a table in this room, made of
ice and piled high with food. Behind the
table sat the Snow Fairy Queen herself.
I could tell she was the Queen because
she was wearing a tall crown made of
upside-down icicles that glimmered and
shimmered whenever she moved her head.

Her skin was white and slightly sparkly like snow but when she smiled I felt warm all the way down to the tips of my toes.

'Hello, Your Majesty,' I said, and did a curtsy like I had been taught to in my ballet lessons. Snow Boy made a flourish and then bowed.

'Who are you?' asked the Queen. She seemed so kind that I didn't feel shy about talking to her.

'My name is Isadora Moon,' I said. 'I am a vampire fairy and this is Snow Boy. I made him in my garden from magic snow and my Aunt Crystal said that I must bring him to the Land of Ice and Snow if I want to stop him melting. So I have

brought him here to you. My aunt said
that even if snow is magic, it always melts
eventually.'

'It does,' agreed the Queen, nodding.
Snow Boy looked frightened.

'Please don't let me melt!' he begged.

'Don't worry,' said the Queen, getting up and putting her arm around him. 'You'll be perfectly safe here.' She gestured towards the table. 'Would you like something to eat after your journey? I was just about to have a little nibble.'

Snow Boy, Pink Rabbit, Snow Bunny, and I sat down at the table with the Queen. There was ice cream cake and peach sorbet and strawberry crushed ice

slush to drink. It was all very delicious.
And very cold. As we ate, we talked. I told
the Queen all about what it was like to
be a vampire fairy and she told us what
it was like to live in the Land of Ice and
Snow. Snow Boy listened in fascination to
everything that we said. He was enjoying
the food too much to speak!

'I must say I am very impressed that you managed to find my palace,' said the Queen. 'It's a difficult place to find. You must be very brave.'

'We used a star map,' I told her. 'I just wanted to help Snow Boy! I couldn't let him melt!'

'Well, you came to the right place,' said the Queen. She turned to Snow Boy and Snow Bunny.

'Would you like to come and live here with me?' she asked them. 'My land is full of people and animals made of snow.'

'I would love that!' said Snow Boy, glancing around at the cold glassy walls of the palace. 'I feel like I belong here!' He

smiled a big wide smile and Snow Bunny
jumped up and down with glee. Then
Snow Boy looked at me and suddenly his
shoulders drooped as though he was a
little sad.

'I will miss you though, Isadora,' he
said. 'You're the best friend I've ever had!'

'I will miss you too, Snow Boy,' I
told him, feeling a lump in my throat.

'But maybe I can come and visit you sometimes?'

'You're welcome here any time, Isadora,' said the Queen. 'But until your next visit, I have a great idea!' She stood up and hurried over to a large chest. Then she opened it and took something out. It was two snow globes, and inside them both were miniature models of her ice palace.

'These are magic snow globes,' she said. 'When you shake them you will be able to see each other and talk!'

'Wow!' I gasped, taking one from her and peering in at the tiny snowy world inside. I had never seen such a beautiful, detailed model before, and when I shook it tiny flakes of snow and glitter swirled down all around the little palace. I shook it a bit harder and Snow Boy's face appeared in the water.

'I can see you!' I said, peering into the globe.

'I can see you too!' laughed Snow Boy.

I looked up and smiled at the Queen. 'I love it!' I said, not feeling quite so sad about saying goodbye to Snow Boy now that we had a way to stay in touch. 'Thank you!'

'You're very welcome,' said the Snow Queen. 'Shall I show you round the palace now?'

'Yes, please!' said Snow Boy and I excitedly.

We all stood up and the Queen led us down sparkling white corridors and up a big grand staircase to the first floor of the palace. Up there was a large room where snow creatures and snow people were playing. Polar bears kicked a snowball round the room, snow dragons flew around the chandeliers, blowing out frosted flakes, and two little snow otters sat at a round table, playing a game of chess made from ice. There was a snow ballerina twirling about in the middle of the floor and a few little snow girls and snow boys running around, playing a game of chase. They all looked very happy and lots of them smiled at us as we passed. Snow Boy raised his hand and waved back. I think he was excited to see other people like him.

'You're new!' shouted one of the snow boys who was kicking a big snowball around the room. He ran over and grabbed Snow Boy's arm.

'I'll show you my favourite thing to do,' he said, beckoning us to all follow him out of the room to the top of a great staircase.

'Watch this,' he said, hopping onto the top of the icy banister and then sliding all the way down.

'Wheee!'

Snow Boy followed suit and after him came Pink Rabbit, Snow Bunny, and me. The Snow Queen watched, smiling.

'I don't want to ruin my dress,' she explained. 'It's stitched together from the finest snowflakes!'

We slid down the banister a few more times and then I stopped and stood back to watch, yawning. Pink Rabbit yawned too because yawns are catching.

'You must be tired,' said the Queen. 'Maybe it's time to head home?'

'I suppose so,' I said reluctantly. I didn't really want to leave. I felt envious of Snow Boy getting to stay in this beautiful sparkling world. But I was very glad he seemed so happy. That was the most important thing.

The Queen led us back downstairs and to the great palace doors.

'It's been so lovely to meet you, Isadora,' she said. 'Thank you for bringing Snow Boy to me. I will take great care of him.'

'That's OK,' I said, yawning again. 'Thank you for the lovely midnight feast!'

The Queen bent down and gave me an icy kiss on the cheek and then Snow

Boy held out his arms and gave me a huge frosty hug.

'Thank you for everything, Isadora,' he said. 'I will miss playing with you. You will always be my very first special friend.

Make sure you look at the snow globe!
And maybe come and visit me some time.'

'I will,' I told him, holding the snow
globe snug against my chest.

I picked Pink Rabbit up, and we
crunched over the snow and climbed back
into the sleigh. I snuggled down under
the blanket and got out the map of the
stars again.

'Goodbye!' I called as the sleigh flew
up into the air.

'Goodbye!' cried Snow Boy. He and
the Queen both waved their hands as
the sleigh rose higher and higher. Snow
Bunny waved her paw too. I looked at
my map and found the first star for

the way back. It shone out brightly,
beckoning me towards home.

Chapter FIVE

It was almost morning by the time we reached my house, but Mum, Dad, and Aunt Crystal had stayed up to wait for me. Mum jumped into the sleigh as soon as it landed and gave me a huge squeezy cuddle.

'How did it go?' she asked. 'Are you OK?'

'I'm fine!' I told her, squeezing back.
'It was wonderful!'

'Well done,' said Mum. 'You've done a great job!'

'It's time for a sleep now though,' said Dad, looking at his watch. 'It's my bedtime too!' He lifted me up and carried me into the house and up to my bed. I fell asleep before my head even hit the pillow and I slept all through the morning and all through lunch. When I woke it was the afternoon.

'What a dream I had!' I said to Pink Rabbit. Then I rubbed my eyes and blinked and remembered that it hadn't been a dream at all. We had gone on an

adventure to the Land of Ice and Snow!
When I got up and looked in the mirror
there was a snowflake on my cheek in
exactly the place where the Snow Queen
had kissed me.

'It will fade over time,' said Aunt
Crystal, when I showed it to her after
bounding into the kitchen for a snack. 'But
it's pretty while it lasts.'

'The snow is still there!' I said, looking out of the window at our white garden. 'Your magic fairy snow!'

'Not my fairy snow anymore,' said Aunt Crystal and pointed beyond the garden to the houses behind, which were now covered in snow too. I gazed up at the sky and saw huge white flakes spinning down towards us.

'It's snowing for real!' said Mum. 'It started while you were asleep.'

I gobbled down a peanut-butter sandwich and then called Zoe, Sashi, Samantha, Dominic, Jasper, and Bruno. I hesitated for a moment and then called Oliver too.

'How was your party?' I asked him.

'Great, thanks,' said Oliver. 'I've saved you some cake and a balloon.'

'Really?' I said. 'That's so nice—thank you!'

'No problem,' said Oliver. 'By the way, it's snowing! Do you want to come and play?'

'That's what I was going to ask you!' I said.

Zoe was first to arrive and we ran out into the garden together, starting to roll balls to make snowmen. I secretly hoped, just a tiny bit, that they would come to life again like yesterday. But deep down I knew they wouldn't. The magic snow had disappeared. After a while Sashi arrived and joined in too, and then Oliver, Bruno, Samantha, Dominic, and Jasper. We started to roll snowballs and throw them at each other, snow splatting all over our coats and down our necks. It was the best snowball fight ever!

Then we
went inside and
Mum melted
a bar of real
chocolate to make

extra thick hot chocolate, and we drank it
with whipped cream and marshmallows
bobbing on top. I nibbled on a piece of
Oliver's birthday cake and looked round
happily at my friends. I missed Snow
Boy—we had had so much fun together—
but I loved my old friends too. The hot
chocolate warmed my whole body and
made me feel all cosy inside. I smiled a
big contented smile. It had been a magical
weekend and I couldn't wait to talk to

Snow Boy through the snow globe that evening. I would treasure the memory of our adventure to the Land of Ice and Snow forever!

Turn the page
for some
fang-tastic
things to make
and do!

Magic snow ice cream

This delicious ice cream will make you feel like you're eating real magic snow!

Ingredients:

★ 8-12 cups crushed ice

★ 300 ml sweetened condensed milk

★ 1 tsp vanilla

Equipment:

☆ Large mixing bowl

☆ Wooden spoon

☆ A grown-up assistant to help

Method:

1. Scoop crushed ice into a large mixing bowl.

2. Add vanilla.

3. Add condensed milk.

4. Stir until well-combined.

5. If necessary, add more ice until you're happy with the consistency of your ice cream.

6. Scoop into a bowl, and enjoy!

7. To freeze leftovers, pat remaining snow ice cream into a freezer-proof container with a lid.

Tingly-toes
hot chocolate

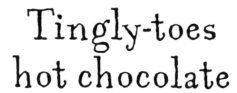

Isadora loves her mum's hot chocolate. It warms
her whole body until her toes feel tingly.

See if this recipe does the same to you . . .

Ingredients:

★ 450ml whole milk

★ 70g 70% cocoa chocolate, finely chopped or grated

★ 30g milk chocolate, finely chopped or grated

★ 75ml single cream

★ Pinch ground cinnamon

★ Pinch of salt

★ Whipped cream

★ Mini marshmallows

Equipment:

☆ Measuring jug

☆ Weighing scales

☆ Grater

☆ Saucepan

☆ Wooden spoon

☆ Whisk

☆ A grown-up assistant to help

Method:

1. Warm about 150ml milk in a pan over a medium heat and stir in the chocolate. Continue to stir until the chocolate has melted into the milk, then whisk in the remaining milk and the cream.

2. Continue to heat until the mixture is hot, but not boiling, then add the cinnamon and a pinch of salt. Taste, adjust if necessary, and serve.

3. For a frothy finish, whisk vigorously just before pouring.

4. Add whipped cream and mini marshmallows to make it super special.

Snowflake biscuits

The perfect accompaniment to tingly-toes
hot chocolate. Not just for snowy days!

SERVES 40

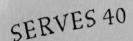

Ingredients:

- ⭐ 350g plain flour, plus extra for dusting
- ⭐ 1 tsp bicarbonate of soda
- ⭐ 1 tsp mixed spice
- ⭐ 125g unsalted butter, chilled and cubed
- ⭐ 2 tsp diced stem ginger in sugar syrup
- ⭐ 175g light brown soft sugar
- ⭐ 1 medium egg, beaten
- ⭐ 14 tbsp golden syrup
- ⭐ 200g icing sugar
- ⭐ 2 tsp edible glitter

Equipment:

- ⭐ 2 baking trays
- ⭐ Baking parchment
- ⭐ Sieve
- ⭐ Mixing bowl
- ⭐ Wooden spoon
- ⭐ Clingfilm
- ⭐ Snowflake pastry cutters
- ⭐ Rolling pin
- ⭐ Drinking straw
- ⭐ Wire rack
- ⭐ Piping bag
- ⭐ A grown-up assistant to help

Method:

1. Preheat the oven to 180°C, fan 160°C, gas 4, and line 2 baking trays with baking parchment.

2. Sift the plain flour, bicarbonate of soda, and mixed spice in a bowl and stir together with a wooden spoon.

3. Rub in the butter until the mixture looks like breadcrumbs.

4. Stir in the ginger, sugar, egg, and golden syrup until you have a firm dough.

5. Turn out onto a lightly floured work surface and knead briefly until smooth.

6. Form into a ball, wrap in clingfilm and chill in the fridge for 15 minutes.

7. Roll out the dough on a lightly floured surface to 5mm thick. Stamp out snowflake shapes with the cutters.

8. Gather the trimmings and repeat step 7 until there is no dough left.

9. Space out well on the baking trays. With the end of the straw, make a hole in the top of each biscuit.

10. Bake for 10–12 minutes until light golden brown. Cool on the trays for 5 minutes, then transfer to a wire rack to cool completely.

11. To decorate, mix the icing sugar and 1-2 teaspoons of water in a bowl until smooth and glossy. The mixture should coat the back of a spoon; add more water if needed.

12. Spoon the icing into the piping bag and snip off the tip to make a small hole. Decorate the biscuits, then sprinkle with edible glitter. Keep in an airtight container for up to 3 days. To hang as decorations, thread thin ribbon through the holes and tie to your Christmas tree.

Raspberry ice lollies

If you're like Snow Boy and you prefer a cold treat, give these tasty raspberry lollies a try!

Ingredients:

★ 300g raspberries

★ 150g strawberries

★ 2 tbsp of icing sugar

★ 200ml of water

Equipment:

☆ Blender

☆ Sieve

☆ Measuring jug

☆ Tablespoon

☆ Lolly moulds

☆ A grown-up assistant to help

Method:

1. Place the berries in a blender with the icing sugar and pulse. Add the water and blend until smooth.

2. Sieve the mixture into a jug, discarding the pips, then pour into sections of a lolly mould tray or into individual lolly moulds. Add the sticks or lids and freeze overnight until firm.

3. Run the mould or moulds under hot water to loosen the lollies, then remove from the moulds.

4. Serve immediately.

Snow globe

Do you want to make your own snow globe, just like Isadora's? We can't promise it will be magic, but it will look magical!

What you will need:

- ⭐ A clean jam jar
- ⭐ White plasticine (optional)
- ⭐ Plastic model trees and festive figures – Christmas cake decorations are perfect for these!
- ⭐ Glitter
- ⭐ Water
- ⭐ Glycerin (available from chemists)
- ⭐ Epoxy resin glue, or any other waterproof glue (available from DIY and craft shops)
- ⭐ A helpful grown up to do some gluing

What to do:

1. Inside the lid of your jar build a snowy hill from the white plasticine (making sure you can still screw the lid onto the jar). This will make it easier to see your little figures.

2. Place the figures and trees on the hill.

3. Ask an adult to glue the hill and figures in place for you, and leave to dry for 15 minutes.

4. Fill the jar with water, almost to the very top. Add two teaspoons of glitter, two drops of glycerin, and stir.

5. Screw the lid tightly back on to your jar.
   Make sure it is on properly, so it does not leak.

6. Turn upside down, gently shake,
   and watch the snow swirl around!

Snowflake window stickers

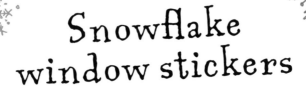

What you will need:

- Pen
- Wax/greaseproof paper
- Fabric paint
- A grown-up assistant to help

What to do:

1. Draw some simple snowflake designs on the paper. Why not use the snowflakes on these pages for inspiration?

2. Carefully trace the lines of your snowflake with the paint. Make sure that the lines are broad and thick—lines that are too delicate may easily break when peeled off from the wax paper.

3. Wait for them to dry—you'll have to be patient, it normally takes at least 24 hours.

4. Stick them to the window! If you have any trouble with them sticking just lightly wipe the back with a damp cloth and try again.

The Freezing Spell Game

To practise her magic, Isadora has brought all her toys to life just for one day. Now she wants to practise her freezing spell.

What you will need:

⭐ An open space

⭐ A magic wand

1. One child is chosen to be 'Isadora', while the rest are the 'toys'.

2. 'Isadora' is given the magic wand and must stand at the far end of the playing area with her back to the 'toys'.

3. While 'Isadora's' back is turned, the 'toys' must walk towards her or him.

4. At any point, 'Isadora' can spin round, point her magic wand at the 'toys', and shout "freeze!"

5. All the 'toys' must stand perfectly still.

6. Any 'toys' that 'Isadora' sees wobbling or moving are sent back to the starting line.

7. The first 'toy' to reach 'Isadora' and tap her or him on the shoulder gets the magic wand and becomes 'Isadora' for the next round.

Writing tips

1. Write Lots

The more you practise, the better you'll get!

2. Read Lots

You'll pick up new techniques and skills by seeing how other writers do it.

3. Write What You Want to Read

Don't worry what other people might think of your story.

All writers started out just like you. Thinking up new ideas and writing stories can be difficult, but the more you practise, the better your stories will be. Even the best and most famous writers all started out as children with pencils and paper practising their stories. So what are you waiting for?

Have fun creating your stories, and I'd love to see them when they're finished! You can share them with me at **harrietmuncaster.co.uk/contact**

Where is your best place to live?

Take the quiz to find out!

What is your favourite thing to eat?

A. Ice cream cake

B. Peanut-butter sandwiches

C. The meal I had for lunch today

What is your favourite thing to do?

A. Slide down slippy bannisters

B. Practise magic

C. Play with my toys

If you could cast a magic spell,
what would you do?

A. Make it snow every day

B. Bring my favourite cuddly toy to life

C. Make Isadora come to my house to play

Results

Mostly As

You should live at the Snow Fairy Queen's palace!
You love running around and having fun in the snow.

Mostly Bs

You should live at Isadora's house! You love using
your imagination and would fit in perfectly
with the Moon family.

Mostly Cs

You should live at your house! You're in just the
right place, you love spending time with your
family and having fun at home.

Harriet Muncaster, that's me! I'm the
author and illustrator of Isadora Moon.
Yes really! I love anything teeny tiny,
anything starry, and everything glittery.

Many more magical stories to collect!

Isadora Moon

Goes to School

Half vampire, half fairy, totally unique!
Harriet Muncaster

Isadora Moon

Goes Camping

Half vampire, half fairy, totally unique!
Harriet Muncaster

Isadora Moon

Has a Birthday

Half vampire, half fairy, totally unique!
Harriet Muncaster

Goes to the Ballet

Half vampire, half fairy, totally unique!
Harriet Muncaster

Goes on a School Trip

Half vampire, half fairy, totally unique!
Harriet Muncaster

Gets in Trouble

Half vampire, half fairy, totally unique!
Harriet Muncaster

Goes to the Fair

Half vampire, half fairy, totally unique!
Harriet Muncaster

ISADORA · MOON

Host your
own magical
Isadora Moon party!

Find a party pack, and lots of
other activities at www.isadoramoon.com